USA Today Bestselling Author

RITA HERRON

Love Me, Lucy

Beachside READS

This is a work of fiction. All incidents and dialogue, and all characters with the exception of some well-known historical and public figures, are products of the author's imagination and are not to be construed as real. Where real-life historical or public figures appear, the situations, incidents and dialogues concerning those persons are entirely fictional and are not intended to depict actual events or to change the entirely fictional nature of the work. In all other respects, any resemblance to persons living or dead is entirely coincidental.

Cover Design by Dayna Linton at Novels Alive TV

Prologue

7 days until Christmas

$\mathscr{A}$LL EMMET ROACH WANTED for Christmas was to break out of jail.

Well, that and to be with the woman he loved.

Lucy Lane.

She was going to be so surprised when he showed up at her door. Maybe he'd wrap himself in a big red bow and drape tinsel all over his body!

Yep, that stupid restraining order hadn't kept him away.

And prison wouldn't either.

His plan was already set. He'd faked a suicide attempt by trying to strangle himself with the garland some idiot guard at the prison had hung in the dining hall to make the room look more festive. Now the doctors had checked him out, he was riding in a prison minivan on his way back to his cell.

His heart raced with excitement and anger as he envisioned Lucy the last time he'd seen her.

He'd tried to convince her that he loved her, that he couldn't live without her, but she'd testified against him and claimed he was stalking her.

This time he would make sure she understood the difference. He wasn't a stalker, he just felt love more intensely than others.

The sound of an engine revving up made him glance in the rearview mirror. His buddy was right on time.

Phase two of his plan was about to begin. The breakout.

He braced himself as his buddy's car roared up, then rammed into the back of the mini-van. The driver cursed, swerved to the right to avoid an oncoming car and struggled to right the vehicle, but his friend rammed them harder and the van's brakes squealed.

The driver lost control, the van skidded, then hit the guardrail and rolled.

Emmet gripped the seat edge to brace himself, but his shoulder jerked with the force of metal hitting asphalt. Then the van skidded upside down into the ravine and careened to a stop against a boulder with a sickening crunch.

The driver's head lolled forward, blood trickling down his forehead. A second later, the van door opened and his friend hauled him through the door.

"Get the damn handcuff key," Emmet hissed.

The driver was trying to rouse, but his buddy whipped open the driver's door, jerked the keys from the key ring on his hip, then unlocked Emmet's handcuffs.

The sweet smell of freedom engulfed him as he tossed the cuffs to the ground and ran toward his buddy's car.

They tore away from the scene, leaving the driver to fend for himself.

"Thanks," he mumbled as a siren wailed past heading toward the wreckage.

A few minutes later, when they both finally stopped checking over their shoulders for the cops, his friend slid a scrap of paper toward him.

Emmet's pulse pounded. "You found her?"

"Yep. She was doing Vegas shows but hooked up with some builder named Reid Summers. Guy and his brother own a construction business in Savannah, Georgia."

Anger churned through his belly. His Lucy was shacking up with some creep after he'd waited for her for the past year?

"Are you sure you want to look her up?" his buddy asked. "You finally got your freedom."

"I'm sure," Emmet said with a sinister smile. "In fact, I can't wait to see her."

This time Lucy wouldn't get away from him.

She loved him, he *knew* it.

He just had to remind her of that fact. Then she would forget the hammerhead and be with him where she belonged.

Maybe they'd even make a baby this Christmas.

And no one would ever tear them apart again.

Yes, it was beginning to look a lot like Christmas...

Chapter One

6 days until Christmas

*R*EID SUMMERS COUNTED THE peppermint sticks in the Christmas countdown calendar Lucy had hung above her bed. Six peppermints left.

Only six days until Christmas.

And he still had no gift.

What in the hell was he going to get Lucy?

She made a cat-like purring sound in her sleep, then rolled over, and he turned on his side to look at her. He loved watching her sleep.

Hell, he loved watching her do anything.

Her fiery red hair lay in a sexy tangle around her face, her lips were swollen from his kisses, and her naked body with its soft curves…looked absolutely delicious.

Damn, he had it bad.

He had never been in love before, but Lucy had blindsided him, and he'd fallen hard and fast for her.

He twirled a strand of her hair around his finger, then pressed a kiss to her cheek. Lucy was surprisingly sweet, funny – and a sex siren whose shocking exotic Vegas showgirl dance act had tied his body in knots the first time he'd seen it. Then last night she'd brought out the sex toys she sold with her Sleepover Inc. business and man, oh, man.

He was sore in places that had never been sore before.

Of course he hadn't known quite what to do with a couple of the contraptions, but hey, he *was* teachable.

Lucy had given up the show life though and was looking for acting jobs, but the image of her in feathers and boas gave him a hard-on every time he thought of it.

Lucy opened her beautiful eyes and smiled. "Morning, lover boy."

Reid's chest pumped up a notch. "Last night was spectacular."

Lucy nodded, then laid a big lip-lock on his mouth. But her cell phone rang a moment later, interrupting them.

"Don't answer it," Reid whispered. "We'll stay in bed all morning, then go to lunch at that shrimp place you like on River Street, then pick up a Christmas tree."

For a brief moment, he considered shopping for an engagement ring to put in her stocking, but he wasn't sure he was ready to go *that* far.

After all, sharing a Christmas tree was sort of a commitment.

Lucy threw the covers aside and reached for her phone on the nightstand. "Sounds wonderful, but this might be my agent."

Reid frowned. He didn't want to lose Lucy to L.A., but he couldn't very well balk at her career choice. He had to be loving and supportive or he'd lose her.

And losing Lucy made him itchy, like he was going to break out in hives.

A small frown puckered Lucy's brow as she studied the number on the caller ID screen. Then she slid from bed and headed to the bathroom. "Be right back."

Reid watched her sashay into the bathroom, already missing her sexy little tush.

Being in a relationship was completely foreign territory to him. His sister Maddie had given him pointers, basically her ten rules to please a woman, so he wouldn't screw up. But he'd frozen up around rule two when she suggested he forget about Sunday afternoon football and give Lucy full reign over his remote.

After all, he was still a bachelor.

In fact, he and his brother Lance and their best friend Chase made a bachelor pact a few years ago, and Lance and Chase had broken the pact when they'd gotten drunk enough on lust and love to get hitched.

His body shuddered as he pictured himself in a monkey suit walking down some aisle and saying words like *forever*. Could he really do it?

Make a commitment to Lucy?

Shoot, what was wrong with him? He *had* made a commitment to her. They were *exclusive*.

Committing didn't have to mean marriage, did it?

LUCY SHIVERED AS SHE closed the bathroom door and answered the call. The man on the other end of the line was the last person she wanted to hear from.

It couldn't be good news.

"Lucy?"

She leaned against the bathroom sink and sighed. "Yes."

"I'm sorry to have to phone."

"What is it, Wallace?"

The two words she'd dreaded hearing the past two years echoed back. "He escaped."

Oh, God. "How?"

"A van crash. Looks like a set up." Wallace sighed in disgust. "Apparently he faked a suicide attempt, was sent to the hospital and was being transported back to jail when it happened."

Lucy chewed her thumbnail. Emmet Roach had made her life a living hell before she'd finally convinced the police that he'd been stalking her. First, he'd befriended her at a Vegas show and she thought he was harmless.

An autograph here. A chance meeting at a coffee shop.

Then it had gotten weird. He'd started following her, sneaking into her apartment and dressing room, stealing her wigs and boas and underwear.

Wearing her wigs and boas and underwear.

The whole situation had gotten downright creepy.

He'd taken it a step farther by trying to kidnap her from a spa when she was getting a bikini wax.

Not only had it been embarrassing, but he'd walked in and told the salon worker exactly how he wanted her landscaped.

She shivered again. He liked his women bald like a baby.

Not that *that* bothered her, but no man told her what to do.

"Lucy," Wallace said. "I know this is not good, but we will find him."

Tears burned the backs of Lucy's eyes. If Emmet had gone to such drastic lengths to escape, he would find her.

"But, Lucy, I think you should go in hiding until we do."

Lucy looked out the window at the Christmas tree lot across the way. Reid was naked and in her warm bed where she wanted to stay. She thought they might shop for a tree together later like a real couple.

Sophie had worked hard to build a new life with Reid's brother Lance.

None of them knew about her situation. About Emmet.

What if he came after one of them to get to her?

"All right," she said. "I'll do it. But not for me. I don't want to endanger anyone I love."

"I understand," Wallace said. "We can put you in a safe house."

Lucy's claustrophobia set in. "I can't be locked up twiddling my thumbs. I'll go crazy." Especially during the holidays when she wanted to be with Reid and her family. And she still had presents to buy!

Besides, since her mother Deseree had quit stripping, attended cosmetology school and started styling wigs for the drag queen show in Savannah, she and Sophie had tried to get together with her at least once a month.

She'd also hoped for a special gift from Santa this year.

"All right. We'll work something else out." Wallace wheezed a breath. "I'll meet you in the Savannah Square in an hour."

Lucy grimaced. A half hour ago, she'd been in blissful heaven with Reid. She wanted to run into his arms now.

But she couldn't tell him what was going on.

Knowing him and his macho overprotective brother, they'd play Tarzan, beat their chests and hunt down Emmet themselves.

She'd have to come up with an excuse to leave town. She couldn't tell Reid the truth or it might put him in danger.

And lordy, lordy, she didn't want him to think she'd encouraged the creep or attracted trouble.

THE SHOWER WATER KICKED on, stirring wicked thoughts in Reid's mind, and he slipped from bed, anxious to join Lucy.

But the bathroom door was locked.

Frowning, he paced to the window and looked out. Last night they'd shared a romantic picnic on the riverbank, then raced back in the rain and made love for hours.

He didn't want the night to end. And today was Sunday…

Sunday usually meant a lazy day reading the paper. He jerked on his jeans and went to retrieve it. Maybe he could talk Lucy back into bed and they could read it together.

The delivery boy had tossed it into the bushes, so he grabbed it and headed back into the kitchen to make coffee. Before he could brew a pot though, the bathroom door opened, and Lucy flitted out in her silky robe. He spied her from the kitchen and rushed to tell her his plan. They'd read the paper together, then he'd serve her breakfast in bed, those croissants she liked with apple butter, and yogurt. And maybe he'd spread a little strawberry jam on her and lick it off…

"Hey, sexy." He dropped the paper on the chaise in the corner, then reached for her.

But Lucy sidestepped him then disappeared into the closet. "Sorry, Reid, but I have to go."

His fantasies wilted. "Go where?"

Lucy yanked out a white t-shirt emblazoned with sparkly angel wings and a pair of jeans then started dressing. "That was my agent. He landed me an audition for a new show they're filming in L.A., and I need to catch a plane."

Just what did this agent guy look like? "This morning?"

She dragged out her suitcase and began to pile clothes in it. "Yes, it's last minute, but a great opportunity. One of those scandalous nighttime soap shows. "And," she added with exuberance, "they already have a big male star signed on."

Just what he wanted to hear.

But he'd be a selfish pig if he asked her not to go because of him.

Hell, if she got the gig, maybe he could find a project for himself out in L.A.

A moment of insecurity struck him. Of course, Lucy might not want him to follow her.

Especially with this big male star she'd be working with around.

"When will you be back?" He frowned as she piled outfit after outfit into the bag. She was taking a lot of clothes. And why did she need those red thongs if he wasn't going with her?

"I don't know," Lucy said as she filled a cosmetic bag with enough assorted lotions and creams to last a month. "It might be a few days. Maybe a week or two."

He glanced at her countdown calendar. "But what about Christmas?"

"Christmas?" Lucy tried to fasten her suitcase, but it was so full the zipper wouldn't budge. She plopped down on it, using her weight to close it. "I can't think about the holidays now, Reid. This part is to die for."

So a part in a show was more important than family and him.

She stuffed his shirt in his hands. "Honestly. Reid. Put on some clothes."

"Not even a quickie before you go?"

She gave his chest the evil eye. "No. I...don't want to miss my flight."

So much for all those crunches he'd done to tone his abs.

Irritated, Reid dragged the shirt on, confused by the change in her demeanor. Lucy was always peppy, fun, up for a good time.

"Don't worry, you'll get there in time. I'll drive you to the airport."

Lucy's eyes flared with something akin to panic. "No, Reid. I'd rather drive myself."

"Why?" He grabbed his belt. "If I drop you off, you won't have to pay for parking."

Lucy shook her head. "No. This way my car will be at the airport when I return."

At least she was planning to return.

She took his arm and pushed him to the door. "Last night was fun. But please leave. I don't need you distracting me."

He pulled her against him and nibbled at her ear. "You didn't mind me distracting you last night."

Lucy whirled away from him, her pretty lips pinched into a scowl.

"Maybe not, but right now I do." She opened the door and shoved him through it. "I've been waiting for this call for months. I can't let anything stand in my way."

Especially him?

Reid started to kiss her again and wish her good luck, but she didn't give him a chance.

She slammed the door in his face.

He stood on the doorstep, bewildered and hurt. Last night they'd whispered words of love while he'd brought her to ecstasy.

This morning he was standing in her way?

Hell, he'd been brushed off before, but never this abruptly. He didn't even know what he'd done wrong.

Maybe she was just looking for fun like you usually do.

And now she had a career break, she was moving on.

He stumbled toward his SUV.

If she landed this part, did that mean it was over between them?

Chapter Two

*L*UCY SWIPED AT TEARS as she watched Reid drive away. Dad blast it,
it had been all she could do not to jump his bones again. Looking at that
naked, sexy chest had almost made her cave.

That stupid Emmet Roach.

It wasn't fair that she had to leave the people she cared about
because he was a lunatic.

But she would do it if it meant protecting Reid and Sophie. After all,
Emmet had been a twittering, nervous, pimple-faced menace before he
went to prison. Being locked up probably hadn't changed him for the
better.

He might even want revenge against her for having him arrested.

She rushed back to her bedroom, grabbed her bags, and hauled them
to her car. A minute later, she hurried back inside, then glanced at her
shoe collection and felt a stab of remorse that she had to leave her
stilettos and Jimmy Choos behind.

She hadn't packed her sexy lingerie either although she had thrown
in those red thongs.

Well, it *was* Christmas and even if no one saw them, she could
fantasize about wearing them for Reid on Christmas day.

Tears clogged her throat, but she swallowed back a sob. No use
blubbering like a baby.

She didn't have time to cry or dwell on what she was missing or the fact that the people she loved might not even miss her.

They *would* miss her, wouldn't they?

Outside, dark clouds gathered, indicating a storm on the way, so she ran back in the apartment for her purse. But the picture of her and Reid at Sophie's wedding mocked her from the end table, and she snatched it up.

Panicked at the idea that Emmet might find her apartment, break in and scour through her things for clues to find her, she made a mad dash through every room, gathering all her personal photos, address book, mail, her I-pad, and the newspaper article featuring Reid and Lance's business and the housing development on Skidaway Island they'd just finished.

She stuffed them all in a tote bag and carried them to her car. She couldn't leave a trail behind for Emmet to follow.

Thunder rumbled as she drove to the square to meet Wallace Bannister, the federal marshal. He was near fifty and had been as close to a father figure as she'd ever had, giving her a shoulder to cry on during the entire Emmet ordeal.

She parked, then followed the sidewalk. Wallace was sitting on a park bench with a newspaper in his lap sipping a cup of coffee, looking very much the casual tourist in his jeans, polo shirt and lightweight jacket. He rubbed a finger across his mustache as she drew near, their signal that it was clear to talk, so she slid onto the bench beside him.

She felt like some spy in a low budget movie that she didn't want to star in.

"Any word on Emmet?" she asked, hoping by some miraculous means the police had caught him and she could keep her holiday plans.

"Afraid not," Wallace said. "But we will get him, Lucy. I promise."

Lucy nodded. She'd been down this road before. There was no telling how long it might take. "So, what's the plan?"

Wallace scanned the area as a young couple pushing a stroller passed. Another man, maybe thirties, wearing a suit paused to smile at Lucy.

She averted her gaze, her nerves spiking. What if Emmet had hired a private investigator to find her? He might have already tracked her down.

She had to get out of town fast.

Wallace waited until the suited man disappeared into the café across the street, then slipped a Manila envelope from inside his jacket. "There's a new ID in here, some cash and a credit card in your new name, along with directions to the place you'll be staying."

Lucy removed the ID and glanced at it. Taylor Overby. Not a bad name. She would have chosen something like Jasmine, but then again that might sound like a stage name and Wallace was careful about his selection. Actually she was surprised he hadn't chosen Smith or Jones.

"Your new wheels are waiting at the Savannah Airport. A beige Buick."

Lucy raised a brow.

"It's about as nondescript as we could find on short notice."

"And absolutely a car I'd never drive," Lucy said, thinking about her lipstick red convertible bug. Now *that* was a car.

"The parking stub shows where it's parked in the long-term lot," Wallace continued. "Leave your car there and take the new one. The space has been paid up for two weeks, but I'll make sure it's updated if we need it."

Two weeks and Christmas would be over.

"The other key is for your condo."

Was he sending her to Alaska or some Podunk little town in the desert? "Where is it?" Lucy asked.

"The Sunset Vista. It's in Delray Beach."

Wasn't that the place Deseree's friend had put her mama in to die? "You're sending me to a nursing care facility?"

"It's not a nursing home, it's a sixties-and-up community." A grin tugged at the corners of Wallace's mouth. "I figured it would be the last place Emmet would look for you."

Lucy shrugged. That was true. It was also the last place she wanted to be during the holidays.

But she would do whatever she had to do until crazy Emmet was caught.

She just hoped that Reid didn't forget her while she was gone.

$\mathcal{R}$EID COULD NOT FORGET the doe-like look on Lucy's face when he'd driven away. Or the curtness in her tone when she'd asked him to leave.

Dammit. He had never allowed a woman to get into his head until her. But Lucy had a way of sneaking up on a man like a cold. Once you caught it, it invaded every pore of your body and left your knees wobbly.

Well, maybe she wasn't *exactly* like a cold…but she definitely made his head foggy and his knees weak.

At a loss as to what to do now that his plans with Lucy had been nixed, he phoned Lance.

The phone rang a half dozen times before his brother finally picked up. "What?"

"How about a game of golf?" He needed to hit something today.

"Since when do you play golf, Reid?"

Lance had a point. "Since I…don't know. I just thought it was a nice day and wanted to be outside."

"Sorry, bro, Sophie and I have plans."

Irrational jealousy hit Reid. Ever since Lance and Chase had gotten hitched, they never wanted to do anything manly. "What? You gonna be Sophie's purse holder while she shops?"

Lance chuckled. "No. We're looking for a Christmas tree."

Exactly what he'd wanted to do with Lucy.

"I thought you and Lucy were keeping each other busy," Lance said.

Reid grunted. "She's flying to L.A. for an audition."

"Really? Well, good for her."

"Yeah, good for her." And bad for him.

"Sophie's calling," Lance said. "We'll catch up at the building site tomorrow."

Reid grunted again, then hung up. Was he going to be whipped like that? Every time Lucy called, he'd run? Hell, Lance practically held Sophie's hand while she peed.

No way. He should view Lucy's trip as a sign that they were on the same page. Have fun, sleep together, but keep their own lives. That was what he wanted.

Wasn't it?

Hell, yeah, it was.

Feeling better, he phoned Chase. Chase might go to a sports bar with him.

"How about we hit the Tavern and watch the game today?" Reid asked.

"Sorry, man, but Maddie and I are buying baby furniture this afternoon. She's already picked out a crib and a baby swing and a bunch of other stuff." Chase lowered his voice. "Oh, and she needs nursing pads and a breast pump. What the hell is that?"

Yikes. He didn't want to know what it was. "I don't know but it sounds painful."

"I know. I hope it's not something I have to help her with," Chase muttered.

Geesh. "TMI, Chase. You're talking about my sister."

"Sorry."

This baby wasn't even here, and it was consuming Chase's life. Soon he'd be talking about spit up and green poop instead of remodeling cars and building houses.

"Well, have fun," Reid said sarcastically.

Chase gave a man grunt. "I know you don't get it now, but you will one day, man."

No way he'd ever go shopping for a breast pump.

Reid said goodbye, then decided to take a run. Maybe he could purge his anxiety with a little sweat.

At least exercise was a masculine activity. And it would keep him in shape. And keep his mind off of the fact that Lucy hadn't invited him to accompany her.

Why would she?

She was going to be hobnobbing with the rich and famous, sipping martinis with male actors who spent more on their hair and clothes than Reid made in a year. She'd become famous and marry some sophisticated L.A. guy who would douse her with riches and diamonds. They'd jet set from country to country, and she'd have her own valet and massage therapist. And one day they'd name a fragrance after her because she smelled so damned erotic that he wanted to drown himself in her scent.

And the only time he'd be able to see her was on the television or big screen where she'd be making out with another man.

$\mathcal{L}$UCY POCKETED THE NEW cell phone Wallace gave her along with her ID and the address for the Sunset Vista and hurried to her car. Christmas decorations adorned the town square and River Street, garland dangling in the breeze from storefronts as she left the downtown area and headed to the airport.

It didn't take her long to find the Buick once she arrived – it stood out like a big beige blob – and would probably fit right into the sixties-and-up scene where she'd be staying.

The wind picked up, swirling leaves around her as she dragged her suitcase from her bug to the Buick.

When she opened the trunk, a nervous giggle escaped her. You could fit at least five bodies in that honker. In fact, her suitcase and cosmetic bag looked pitiful, lost, as if she should go back and pack more.

A few of her strappy sandals and those gorgeous black pumps...

No, you need to get out of town, Lucy. Emmet might be staking out your apartment now.

She quickly exchanged vehicles, loading up her clothes and photos. She had never been to Delray Beach, but she'd heard it was a nice little town right on the beach and intracoastal waterway with tons of shopping and restaurants.

Of course, she wouldn't enjoy any of that because she'd be looking over her shoulder for Emmet.

The first raindrops splattered the windshield as she pulled from the parking lot. Wallace knew she was disastrous at directions, so thankfully he'd managed to find her a car with a built-in GPS. The moment she started the engine, the address and directions for Delray popped on the screen.

"Turn right from the parking lot," the voice control said.

Lucy patted the dash. If this faceless voice was going to be her only company for the next few hundred miles, she might as well give her a name. "Got you, Jenny Lou."

Jenny Lou didn't respond so she sped down the highway, chatting to her as she drove. By the time she passed into Florida, she was missing Reid terribly and imagining Emmet rolling around naked in the sheets where she and Reid had made love.

He was just sick enough to do that.

"I don't know what to do about Reid, Jenny Lou. What if he never wants to get married?"

Jenny Lou was a good listener, but she had zilch advice in the romance department.

Her cell phone buzzed and she checked the number. Reid.

She groaned. She needed to hear his voice. To know that some other woman wasn't raking her hands over those iron-taut abs.

She wanted to explain why she'd run him off this morning like she had a bee up her butt.

But she forced her hand to remain on the steering wheel. If she confessed the truth, Reid would insist on coming along to protect her and that would be dangerous.

Besides, if Emmet somehow discovered that she and Reid were involved, and tried to force him to reveal her location, Reid couldn't tell him if he didn't know.

It was better he believe she was on an audition, instead of running from a nut who liked to smell her underwear and thought she was the reincarnation of his dead wife.

 *E*MMET BYPASSED LUCY'S apartment then parked the car he'd stolen down the street. He had to be careful. Didn't want to attract unwanted attention.

Not since he was an escaped con.

Damn Lucy for putting him in this position.

His fingers tingled as he imagined finally being able to touch her again.

Had she thought about him the last few months?

Maybe she'd realized that he hadn't been stalking her, that he *loved* her like no other man could. That they were made for each other, just like she'd told him in her first life.

His eye twitched, a rash exploding across his neck as he pulled himself from the driver's side and walked down the street. He forced himself not to claw at the red bumps. He wanted to look his best when Lucy saw him.

Was she home now? Did she know he was out of prison?

A black sedan parked across the street caught his eye, and he tugged the ball cap he'd worn as a disguise lower over his head. What if the police were watching, waiting to trap him?

He scanned the street again. Yep, someone was in that black sedan.

He rubbed at his neck, darted between two houses, then cut between their back yards. A red wagon and tricycle suggested children inhabited the house, but the lights were off, indicating the family wasn't home.

He suddenly imagined having a child with Lucy and excitement zinged through him. Yes, as soon as they were together again, he'd suggest they start making a baby, a little Emmet, Jr. Or a lovely little Lucy girl with red curls.

Ducking low, he crept along the red-tips and crossed the next yard until he reached Lucy's. He hid behind a potted plant, watching, waiting, checking to make sure some idiot cop wasn't lying in wait like a rabid animal ready to pounce.

Speaking of dogs, a little mutant throwback dog with wiry hair barked, then raced down the deck steps of the neighbor's house and ran toward him.

Panicked, Emmet jogged toward Lucy's back porch, jumped over a lounge chair and dove toward the door. He wiggled the doorknob, but the door was locked.

The dog's yappy bark echoed closer, and Emmet fumbled and dropped his lock-picking device.

He quickly retrieved it, sweating as he picked the lock.

But just as he thought he was home free, the damned dog leaped at him and sank his teeth into Emmet's ass.

Chapter Three

*L*UCY MADE IT TO the Sunset Vista with only a few minor

complications. She and Jenny Lou had bickered a few times. Really, couldn't they have designed the woman to carry on a conversation instead of just drone out directions?

At least Jenny Lou hadn't failed her when Lucy took a wrong turn and nearly wound up headed to Tampa instead of Delray. Then she'd had a flat tire in the rain, but a sweet little teenage boy and his buddy with the alligator tattoo had stopped to help her, although judging from their eyes and the way they giggled as they dropped the lug nuts in the mud, they were high on weed. When she'd offered to pay them, they'd said it had been worth it.

Then she'd noticed her white t-shirt plastered to her chest and realized she looked like a contestant in a wet t-shirt contest.

Thankfully she'd left the rain behind at the state line, and after she'd gotten on the Florida Parkway, she'd stopped to pee and get something to eat. But the only thing left in the station was a rubbery piece of pizza that had looked questionable and tasted like cardboard.

It wasn't sitting too pretty in her stomach either.

Swallowing back the queasy feeling, she parked in front of the lobby/main office and hitched herself out. The Sunset Vista was a group of condos set on the intracoastal waterway with pink flamingos wearing Santa hats decorating the neatly kept lawn.

A white-haired man in a pale blue suit approached her with a twinkle in his eye when she entered. "Can I help you, Miss?"

Lucy nodded. "My name is L…Taylor Overby."

"Yes, yes," the man said. "I'm A.J. Moon, but folks call me Moon. We're so excited you came! We've wanted a social coordinator for a long time."

A social coordinator? She'd assumed she'd be doing some office work, filing, answering the phone. "You have?"

Moon winked at her. "Yes, we're seniors, not dead, honey. We like to kick up our heels and have fun."

She spied his walker and bit her tongue.

"I was a dancer in my time," he said with a grin. "I can still cut a rug with my cane."

Lucy laughed in spite of herself, then hooked her arm though his as he gave her the tour.

"This is the office and the mail room where residents pick up packages," he said, using his cane as a pointing stick.

"You're probably swamped with Christmas gifts and cards right now," Lucy said.

Moon's face fell slightly. "Some people get mail, but there are others whose families are just too busy for them."

Lucy's chest ached. "Well, we'll have to fix that. Maybe we can draw names and exchange Secret Santa gifts."

"That's a great idea." Moon squeezed her arm. "I think we're going to like having you around."

He led her to a larger room that resembled a sports bar with a giant flat screen TV and cozy seating nooks. A few men had gathered to drink beer and watch the football game.

"We meet here for ball games, movies, Bridge tournaments, Bingo, craft club and other events," Moon said.

A small woman with silver hair sat nursing a cup of coffee as she hovered over the newspaper in the corner.

"That's Mae," Moon said. "She reads the obits every day hunting for a husband. Soon as a man's wife passes, she bakes him a pie." He smiled. "The minute you smell blueberries around here, you know someone bit the dust."

Lucy bit back another laugh as he introduced her.

Mae clapped her hands, her eyes lighting up. "Can we start a Zumba class? And how about yoga?"

"Sure. We can do both." She could use her dance moves and stay in shape while she was here.

In Vegas, they planned a special Christmas show every year, too. "Maybe we can put on a talent show for Christmas Eve."

"Oh, my gosh, that sounds like fun." Mae gathered her paper and coffee cup. "I'm going to tell some of the others right now!"

She waved and ran off, then Moon showed her the workout room and pool which had been built on a massive deck that overlooked the inlet. A couple of women were sipping drinks as they watched the sunset while another couple huddled together on a lounge chair, their hands entwined.

"They've been married fifty years," Moon said. "Me, I was a bachelor, never did settle down."

A pang of longing for Reid welled inside Lucy as she watched the couple kiss. Sophie had told her that Reid, Lance and Chase had once signed bachelor pacts vowing they'd never get married.

Would Reid tear his up for her, or was he committed to being single?

3 days until Christmas

*T*HREE LONG DAYS HAD passed and no word from Lucy.

Reid was going out of his mind. Why in the hell hadn't she called?

He grabbed a vitamin water and chugged it down. The renovation on the Tybee house looked terrific. In fact, he'd put overtime in this week, pounding out his frustration with a hammer and nails, and was ahead of schedule.

He checked his phone but there were no messages.

Irritated, he punched Sophie's number. Her morning talk show should be over now, so hopefully he'd catch her at a good time.

She answered on the fourth ring. "Hello, it's Sophie."

"Reid," he said without preamble. "Have you heard from your sister?"

A second passed. "No, why?"

Reid scrubbed a hand over his face. Would he sound too damn needy if he asked?

He was going to ask anyway. "I'm worried," he admitted. "She left three days ago for an audition in L.A. and she hasn't called."

Sophie sighed. "Reid, you know Lucy. She's probably shoe shopping or maybe her agent set up several auditions. She probably doesn't want to call until she knows she got the part."

And if she did, she'd never come back.

"She will be back for Christmas, won't she?" Reid asked.

"Of course," Sophie said. "Deseree is coming, and we're all meeting at Maddie and Chase's house."

Relief surged through Reid. He didn't know why his gut had been churning since Lucy had left, but he had a bad feeling something wasn't right.

Was this Lucy's way of blowing him off?

If it was, maybe he should just accept it. He liked being a bachelor. He would go back to his single life.

Bar hopping. Dating a different girl every night. Having sex with one girl one day and then jumping into bed with another.

A cold sweat broke out on him. Except suddenly he didn't want to move on or sleep with anyone but Lucy.

*H*E WAVED GOOD NIGHT to his crew as they left, then jumped in his SUV and drove toward Lucy's. Maybe she'd come home early and was just jet lagged and had crawled into bed to catch up on her sleep.

And if not, he'd pick up a Christmas tree and decorate it as a surprise for her when she returned. If they waited any longer, the good ones would be gone.

A half hour later, he parked at her house, disappointed when he didn't see her car in the driveway. The house was dark, too. He climbed out, then untied the tree from the roof of his SUV and dragged it up to the front door.

Lucy was notorious for losing keys, so she had several hidden outside. He dug the spare key from beneath the plastic Snowman in the front yard, then let himself in, hauled the tree into the den and set it up in front of the window.

Then he retrieved the box of ornaments and lights from his trunk and brought them in.

Lucy usually kept the radio playing, and Vegas show tunes wafted from the upstairs. Had she left the radio on when she left?

He could see her dancing in that nothing of a costume she'd worn in the Diva act. Even at home, Lucy was always moving, fluid, graceful sexy moves that made him hard just thinking about them.

A sound jarred him, and he frowned and went to the kitchen to see what it was. The back door was cracked slightly, wind whistling in.

That was odd. Had Lucy forgotten to lock it?

Then he noticed that the stove eye was red. He checked the knob, but the oven was off. Still, it felt warm.

Which meant someone had been here recently.

Lucy?

Had she come home and not called him?

Maybe she was upstairs…

Curious, he climbed the steps to the bedroom, then paused at the sight of the unmade bed. The sheets looked tangled, the comforter thrown off as if someone had been romping around in bed.

Like it did when they made love.

Several silk nightgowns, panties and bras were also spread across the sheets.

His gut tightened as he realized the obvious. Lucy *had* been home…

But where was she now?

A low light glowed from the bathroom. Maybe she was bathing, then she planned to pick out the teddy she wanted to wear when she called him and invited him over.

His blood running hot at the thought, he crossed the room and opened the door. The tub was filled with bubble bath, flower petals floating on top, but Lucy wasn't in the room.

Then his gaze swept the romantic set up. Candles glowed from the windowsill and two half full wine glasses sat on the table next to the claw foot tub.

Disappointment ballooned in his chest.

Dammit, he'd snuck in to surprise her, but she'd pulled one over on him.

She hadn't left town at all.

She'd been here all along — entertaining another man.

*E*MMET BACKED HIMSELF inside Lucy's closet, hiding behind a rack of dresses as he listened to the footsteps inside her bedroom. The scent of her body lotion clung to the satin sheaths and feather boas dangling in his face. He pressed a fluffy red boa to his cheek, drowning himself in her exotic smell. He couldn't resist trying on the black spangled stilettos on the floor.

By God, they were sexy. And they made his feet look so small…

A noise sounded, startling him back to reality, and he peered through the crack in the door and spotted a dark-haired muscular guy in jeans and a denim shirt looking at the underwear he'd spread across Lucy's bed. Was this the low rent carpenter she'd hooked up with?

The man touched one of the silky teddies and Emmet's blood boiled.

How dare he touch Lucy's underwear. He should be hanging off a ladder repairing other people's roofs or on his belly fixing toilets, not in her house!

A sneeze tickled his nose, but he pressed the feathers into his face to stifle it while he waited on the man to leave. Then a thought struck him.

He'd been here three days waiting on Lucy to return. If this creep was Lucy's boyfriend, maybe he would lead him to Lucy.

Then he'd get rid of the competition and Lucy would be his.

Chapter Four

THREE MORE DAYS UNTIL Christmas. Lucy missed Reid more every day that passed.

But she tried to focus on her new friends at Sunset Vista.

The fact that their families were either gone or were too busy to include them in their plans broke her heart.

Just as Deseree had so many times.

She would not let the Silver Sneakers, the women who walked every morning on the beach, down.

Pasting on a smile, she entered the common room, laden with decorations. Some of the men had already strung colorful, twinkling Christmas lights across the room, and another resident had decorated the doors with angels and wreaths. Santas and snowmen stood out against the palm trees outside.

Her phone buzzed on her hip, and she checked the number. Reid and Sophie had each left a dozen messages.

She set the box on the table and the Silver Sneakers attacked it, grabbing ornaments and mistletoe and tinsel and giggling as they discussed the upcoming talent show.

She stepped aside to listen to Sophie's message wishing she could talk to her and tell her about this place.

"Lucy, call me," Sophie said. "I'm counting on you being home for Christmas. Deseree is actually talking about cooking this year."

Lucy blinked back tears. She wanted to be there with them and see *that.* But she couldn't bring Emmet into her sister's life, not when Sophie had finally found happiness.

The room grew noisy as more residents filed in for the tree decorating party. Christmas t-shirts were the theme since it was too warm for sweaters, and Moon handed out Santa hats.

Birdie, the matchmaker of the Silver Sneakers, stood instructing Able Cooligan, her current boyfriend, strategic places to hang the mistletoe to optimize kissing opportunities for the singles.

"Our bodies might be sagging and bagging," Birdie said as she pointed to her wrinkly knees and winked. "But inside we're still the same."

Lucy hugged the woman. "Everything looks great."

Mae strolled in wearing a reindeer shirt, and Lucy detected the smell of blueberries. "Have you been baking?"

Mae blushed. "I'm making a cobbler to take to a man from my church whose wife just passed. I just saw the obit this morning."

"It would be awful to lose a loved one during the holidays," Lucy said. It was bad enough just being separated.

"I know. It's so sad." She dabbed at her eyes. "But there's a whole pew of widow women who've been eying him," Mae said with a nervous frown. "He probably has casseroles up to his eyeballs."

"I'm sure your pie will be the best," she told the sweet woman.

"I don't know, Ellen made him her sour cream coconut cake. Everyone says it's better than sex."

Lucy grinned. She wanted a piece of that cake.

Mae patted her gray curls. "You think I should get highlights to make me look younger? Or maybe we should have a Botox party."

Lucy shook her head. "No, you are beautiful just the way you are."

Moon and three of the men adjusted the tree in the tree stand while Rhoda, a woman who wore diamonds on every hand, directed them, her bangled bracelets jangling.

"To the right a little. No, no, now to the left."

The group had bickered about where to put the tree at first, then how much to cut off the bottom. She'd finally stepped in to settle the dispute and now the tree stood by the picture window that offered an impressive view of the pool and intracoastal waterway.

In another corner, seventy-year-old DeEtte, one of the quilters of the bunch and the leader of the Silver Sneakers, taught a group how to make Christmas ornaments from the seashells they'd collected on their morning walk.

Flora, a spry eighty-year-old who suffered slight memory lapses and constantly forgot her teeth, filled candy jars with red and green M & M's, placing them around the room while Billy and Nelda, the couple who'd been married so long, erected a manger scene on the front lawn.

Lucy spied the table where several Secret Santa gifts waited to be picked up. Since most of the residents were on a budget, she had instigated a ten-dollar limit on presents. So far, the group had loved their surprises and were constantly whispering, wondering who'd drawn their name.

Their five o'clock cocktail hour began, and Sue, a smart real estate saleswoman, passed out holiday martinis complete with peppermint chips floating on top. Lucy flipped her ipod to a Christmas playlist and snapped pictures as the group decorated the tree.

"Tomorrow morning we start practicing for our holiday talent show," Lucy said. "Start thinking about what you want to do. We want everyone to have a part."

"I don't have a talent," Ellen said.

"Yes, you do," Nancy, a woman who dyed her hair blue said. "You can sew."

"That's perfect," Lucy said. "You can make the costumes and sets!"

Moon sat down at the piano and began to pick out *White Christmas*.

Inez, a seventy-year-old who was proud of her two new hips, passed out jingle bells, and they all joined in and began to sing.

Mae sidled over to Lucy. "You know what, hon. There's a secret Santa gift over there with your name on it."

Lucy tensed. "But I didn't put my name in the stocking."

Mae shrugged. "Maybe you have a secret admirer."

Lucy's stomach fluttered. Emmet used to leave her little presents all the time when he'd been stalking her.

Lord help her. Surely he hadn't found her here.

$\mathcal{D}$AD BLAST IT. LUCY was two-timing him.

Reid surveyed her bedroom again, stunned. Sure, he hadn't exactly proposed to Lucy or bought her a ring, but he thought things had been going well.

How could he have been so wrong?

Lucy was fun loving and flirty and had been a dancer in Vegas, but would she really hop from his bed to another man's?

His cell phone buzzed, and he checked the number. Sophie.

Maybe she knew what was going on. He quickly punched connect. "Sophie?"

"Reid, have you heard from Lucy?"

"No. Have you?"

A tense heartbeat passed. "No. I've left several messages but she hasn't returned my calls."

Worry knotted his belly. Sophie sounded anxious, not a good sign. "I'm at her apartment now," Reid admitted. "I dropped by the house to surprise her with a Christmas tree when she returned, but she's not here. Although it looks like she has been."

"What are you talking about?" Sophie said.

"The kitchen stove was warm, and Lucy's underwear is strewn all over her bed. There are two wine glasses by the bathtub with a bubble bath waiting, too. A *fresh* bubble bath."

"Are you sure?" Sophie asked.

Reid scrubbed a hand over his chin. "I'm not making this up. It looks like she's been entertaining. There are damn flower petals floating in the bath water."

"I don't understand," Sophie said. "Lucy wouldn't cheat on you, Reid."

What other explanation could there be?

Sophie's soft sigh echoed back. "Maybe she let a friend stay at her apartment."

Reid considered that possibility. "I suppose she could have, but there isn't a car here." He walked through the room, checked the bathroom, then looked inside the closet. Shoes were scattered on the floor.

Odd. Lucy prided herself on her shoes and kept them in the shoeboxes or the little gloved cases the boutiques wrapped them in as if they were gold.

His gaze scanned the closet again. A pair of black lace panties lay on the floor, torn in the crotch.

"Reid?" Sophie asked.

"I don't see a suitcase. If a friend is staying here, wouldn't they have brought an overnight bag?"

"Probably," Sophie said, sounding worried.

"And Lucy's closet...it's a wreck. Her shoes are everywhere."

"You're right. Something's wrong," Sophie said. "Let me call you back in a second. I'll call her agent and see where she's staying."

Reid breathed deeply. "Good. I'll feel better if I know she's safe."

Because if she wasn't here or hadn't loaned her place to a friend, someone had broken in, pawed through her clothes and made himself at home.

A siren wailed in the distance, and Reid decided to look around downstairs. Maybe Lucy had left a notepad with the name of her hotel.

His phone buzzed again, and he punched connect. "Sophie?"

"Reid, Lucy's agent said he never called her for an audition."

Reid heaved a sigh. "Then she's dumping me."

"We don't know that," Sophie said. "Besides, if she was, she would have told me. And she's not returning my calls either."

Now he was worried. The siren wailed closer, and he jogged down the stairs.

"I'll call you if I hear from her," Sophie said, then the phone went dead.

Just as Reid reached the foyer, the front door burst open and a roly-poly policeman rushed through the door, his gun drawn. "Police, don't move."

Reid froze and threw his hands up in surrender. What the hell?

A noise sounded from the kitchen, footsteps pounded, and another officer barreled around the corner, his gun drawn. "You're under arrest!"

Reid swallowed hard. "What's going on?"

The officer grabbed his arm. "Turn around and spread 'em."

Reid choked back a curse as the officer shoved him against the wall.

"Why are you arresting me?" Reid asked as the cop frisked him.

"Breaking and entering for starters."

"I didn't break in, my girlfriend lives here."

"Yeah, right," the officer growled.

"It's true," Reid said. "Just call her and she'll tell you." Of course, she'd have to answer the damn phone first.

"Shut up and walk to the car," the second officer snapped. "You can tell it all to the judge."

Cop one frowned. "Not that it will do any good, buddy. Stalking a woman is serious stuff."

"Stalking?" Reid asked. "I'm not stalking Lucy, I'm in love with her."

"Uh-huh," Roly-poly muttered. "We've heard that before."

"It's true," Reid said. "I love Lucy."

"Yeah," cop two said. "Stalking all right. Poor woman."

Poor woman. She'd lied to him. Who knows where she was. She might be playing touchy-feely between the sheets with some other man, while he was being arrested for trying to surprise her with a Christmas tree.

"Please," he said, vying for calm. "You have to listen, let me explain."

"You can explain what you did to Lucy," cop one said as the second cop raced up the steps. "Where is she?"

"I told you; I don't know," Reid said between clenched teeth.

"Right," cop one said as he twisted his arm. "Listen, buddy, we'll go easier on you if you just confess."

"Confess to what?" Reid barked.

"To stalking and kidnapping," the cop said.

"That's crazy," Reid said. "I'm telling you, Lucy is my girlfriend and — "

"You are sick," cop one muttered beneath his breath.

What? Reid's shoulders snapped back as the guy pushed him toward the door. "You're making a mistake."

Cop two rushed down the steps, his jowls jiggling. "Nothing upstairs. But it looks like the freak has been wallowing in her underwear on the bed."

"I have not," Reid bellowed.

"Shut up, you pervert," cop number two growled. "I hate your kind. You probably can't even get it up."

Panic mingled with anger making Reid want to spit. But common sense kicked in and warned him that wouldn't be a good idea.

Then cop one dragged Reid onto the front lawn where blue lights twirled against the darkness. "You're going to be sorry," he muttered as the officer shoved his head down and pushed him in the back seat.

"That sounds like a threat," cop two mumbled.

"Damn right it does," the other cop said. "Let's add threatening an officer to the charges."

Reid gritted his teeth as the officer slammed the car door. Dad blast it, he'd keep his mouth shut until he reached the police station. Then he'd demand his phone call and figure out what the hell was going on.

And why these bozos thought he was stalking Lucy.

EMMET PRESSED THE BOA over his mouth to stifle a laugh as the police car roared away.

Did that bastard really think Lucy loved him when she belonged to Emmet?

At least the cops had taken care of the smuck. Obviously hammerhead didn't know where Lucy was or he would have called her to verify his story.

A stroke of luck for *him*.

Except he still had no idea where Lucy was.

He slipped from the closet, Lucy's boa wrapped around his neck.

He had to find her before the cops realized they had the wrong guy.

He grabbed his phone and sprawled on her bed, draping her underwear over him.

"The police must have alerted Lucy," he told his friend when he answered. "I think she left town. I need a trace on her phone."

"Are you sure you want to go that route?"

"Just do it," he said impatiently.

His buddy made a clicking sound with his teeth. "All right. You should know something by tomorrow."

Emmet ended the call, then found a local reporter's name from the newspaper on the table and called the number. A young woman named Jewel. She was probably hungry for a story.

"I have an anonymous tip," he said. "Police just arrested a stalker at the home of Lucy Lane."

"Who is this?" Jewel asked.

"I don't want my name mentioned, but I witnessed the arrest myself. The man's name is Emmet Roach. He escaped prison and broke into Lucy's house."

"Thanks," Jewel said. "I appreciate the information."

"Good, I'm sure Miss Lane wants to know she can come home for Christmas."

He dropped the phone in its cradle, then closed his eyes and imagined being with Lucy.

She'd wear the red lace teddy trimmed in white lace, the one he'd put in her stocking. He'd dress like Santa Claus and pretend to come down the chimney, then they'd strip, and he'd dribble eggnog on her belly and lick it off.

Then they'd make love on the floor in front of the fireplace.

Everything would be perfect. They'd get married and welcome the new year as man and wife.

Yep, Santa was finally coming to see him this year. It was going to be a jolly, jolly Christmas and a happy new year!

Chapter Five

$\mathcal{R}$EID STRUGGLED TO REMAIN calm as he was fingerprinted, processed and tossed into jail.

Lance was going to kill him.

He'd seen the inside of a cell when he was a teenager, but that was half a lifetime ago when he'd been angry and rebellious.

Now he had a business with his brother and was respected in the community. If his arrest got out, it could cause problems for their company.

A prisoner in the next holding cell banged on the bars, ranting about aliens while two drunks in the cell next to him demolished Ninety-nine Bottles of Beer on the Wall with their slurred singing.

Reid gripped the bars and bellowed his innocence. "Give me my phone call. I'm innocent."

"Shut up," the alien guy said.

He yelled again, but no one came. Dammit, why wouldn't they listen to him?

Did he look like a crazed stalker?

The tattooed skinhead in the cell with him played drums on his legs with his hands while a cross-dresser in a Mrs. Santa outfit whined in the corner, insisting he hadn't been soliciting in front of the fancy B & B where he'd been picked up.

It was going to be a long damn night.

He stared at the clock and paced the cell. But as the minutes rolled into hours and midnight struck, his mind traveled down a dark path.

If the police thought he was stalking Lucy, they had a reason. The fact that she'd rushed him away added to his anxiety.

Come to think of it, he hadn't actually seen her leave her apartment.

What if something had happened to her?

He mentally reviewed the facts. She was upset after that phone call the other morning. And tonight, her clothes and shoes had been scattered all over the place as if someone had rifled through them. As if someone was staying there.

Either Lucy was cheating on him, or she was…in trouble.

He gripped the bars of the cell and yelled for the guard. He just couldn't sit in this cell and rot if Lucy needed him.

"I need my phone call," he yelled again.

The skinhead next to him laughed. "Good luck with that one, buddy. They usually make you wait twenty-four hours."

Twenty-four hours?

Reid yelled again and banged on the bars until his voice was hoarse. But the skinhead was right.

No one came.

Finally he sank onto the floor in the corner and closed his eyes. He'd tough it out tonight, but in the morning, they'd better give him his call.

He just hoped something bad hadn't happened to Lucy.

*L*UCY LAUGHED AS THE women gathered around, listening to Ellen read sex tips from a book on sex for seniors that she'd received in her Secret Santa gift bag.

"Do you have a boyfriend, Taylor?" Sue asked.

Lucy polished off her peppermint martini. "Well, yes, I do."

"What is he like?" DeEtte asked.

"I bet he's a hunk with a six-pack," Nelda said.

"Yeah, and not one with Bud's name on it," Ellen joked.

"Are you two doing the deed?" Mae asked.

Lucy laughed. "You mean sex?"

Willene narrowed her eyes. "You don't have to get personal, Mae. Just because getting laid is all you think about doesn't mean everyone else thinks about it all the time."

"I wished men thought about it more," Sue mumbled.

"Of course they're doing it," DeEtte said. "All the young folks do it."

"You know what they say about not buying the cow if you've had the milk," Ellen said.

"That's just old fashioned," Mae said.

"Taylor?" DeEtte said. "Is he good to you? I mean does he *satisfy* you?"

Lucy blushed. "Well, yes, he does," she said, remembering the wicked things he did with his tongue. "It's just…I don't know if he wants to ever get married."

"Oh, no, one of those commitaholis," Sue offered.

"*Commitaphobics*," Ellen corrected.

"You have to give them a little incentive," Mae said.

Willene frowned. "I don't think baking pies works for the young kids."

"My coconut cake gets me some loving every time, " Ellen said.

Inez made a tsking sound to Ellen. "But we're talking about marriage, not getting someone in the sack."

Nelda raised her eyebrows and winked. "Honey, the secret is to keep him guessing."

Ellen murmured Amen. "Yep, keep him fed and sexed up, and he'll be faithful."

Lucy fidgeted. All this talk about sex only made her ache for Reid. "Thanks for all the advice, ladies, but I'm going to turn in now." Although she might ask Ellen and Mae for their recipes later. She had conquered the sex thing, but she couldn't cook worth a damn.

"Don't forget your Secret Santa bag," Mae said as Lucy stood.

Lucy eyed it as if she thought spiders might crawl out of it any minute, but retrieved it and headed to the door.

The women dispersed, agreeing that Ellen would pass her new book around when she was finished.

The clock struck midnight, and Lucy scanned the Sunset Vista property as she carried the Secret Santa bag back to her unit.

Everyone in the group had a Secret Santa except her.

So who had left her a gift?

She checked over her shoulder again, then let herself inside the condo and flipped on the light. Nerves skittered through her as she scanned the living room/kitchen combination. Everything looked the same. The plain beige walls and sofa, the bowl of fruit Wallace had ordered to be sent to the condo, the painting of the seashore, and the calendar that reminded her how many days she'd been gone.

And how many days until Christmas day.

Frustrated that Wallace hadn't caught Emmet, she checked the bathroom and bedroom. Her underwear drawer was closed. A good sign Emmet hadn't been here.

The photo she'd brought with her of Reid stared at her from the bedside table. Tears threatened, but she swallowed them back.

Wallace would catch Emmet soon. He had to. Then she could go home and everything would be all right.

Resigned, she walked back to the kitchen, fixed herself a cosmo, then pushed the tissue paper in her gift bag aside. Surprise stole through her as she lifted a slinky red halter dress from inside.

A card fluttered to the floor, and she picked it up and read it.

A pretty dress for a beautiful woman.

A shiver rippled through her. It was exactly the type of sexy dress Emmet would have chosen.

Had he found her?

Her finger shook as the punched Wallace's number. He didn't answer, so she left a message.

"Call me. I have to know if Emmet's found me."

Her hand trembled as she stuffed the dress back inside the bag.

Then she carried her drink to her patio. A cruise boat sailed by, Christmas lights twinkling. Voices and laughter drifted to her in the breeze. A party was on board, Christmas carols wafting through the air.

Lucy had never seen anything so beautiful in her life.

But she had never been so lonely either.

Twice she'd walked along Venetian Drive down to Atlantic and strolled the streets, which were filled with tourists and locals enjoying the coffee shops and restaurants. She'd even gotten a little shopping in.

Yet each step she'd taken, she'd searched the crowd for Emmet, afraid he was watching her.

Even now, she couldn't help but wonder if he was lurking in one of those small fishing boats docked along the pier.

2 days until Christmas

$\mathcal{R}$EID WOKE TO THE sound of a rhinoceroses growling. No, a pack of them.

A symphony of similar sounds roared through the cellblock, reminding him he hadn't spent the night in his own bed.

That he'd been arrested for stalking the woman he loved.

It was also Christmas Eve, he had no gift for Lucy, and not a clue where she was.

Footsteps clattered, the sound of a baton banging the cell doors echoing, then a guard stopped in front of him. "Reid Summers. Come with me. A federal marshal wants to talk to you."

Reid's heart tripped a beat. A federal marshal?

Keys jangled as the guard unlocked the cell door and gestured for Reid to go with him. Reid followed beside the man, reminding himself to remain calm.

If he acted like a crazed person, they'd lock him back up.

Five minutes later he was seated in an interrogation room, his handcuffed hands splayed on the table. A low light hung over the scarred table, the room bare except for the table and three straight chairs.

He tapped his foot on the floor while he waited, straightening when a tall silver-haired man entered. His face looked slightly haggard, his eyes steely gray.

"Mr. Summers," he said. "My name is Marshal Bannister."

"What's going on?" Reid asked.

Marshal Bannister folded his arms. "What were you doing in Lucy Lane's apartment?"

Frustration knotted every muscle in Reid's body. "She's my girlfriend."

The marshal's eyes flickered with interest. "Is that so?"

"Yes," Reid said. "We've been dating for the past few months."

"Hmm." The marshal studied him. "She didn't mention you to me."

"Why would she?" Reid asked. For cripes sake, surely Lucy wasn't two-timing him with this crusty codger.

Marshal Bannister leaned forward. "Listen, Mr. Summers, this is serious. According to the police, you broke in and Miss Lane's clothing and shoes had been strewn across her bed and closet."

"First of all, Lucy showed me where she keeps the spare key," Reid said. Although come to think of it, why hadn't she given him a key? Because she didn't want him catching her with another man? "And second, I didn't make that mess."

"When did you last see Lucy?"

Reid mentally counted back the days. "Six days ago. I spent the night with her, then she claimed she received a phone call from her agent saying he'd scheduled an audition for Lucy. She packed in a hurry and I left. I haven't heard from her since."

"So what were you doing at her place last night?"

He hesitated. If Lucy was trying to dump him, he was going to look like a big damn fool.

"Mr. Summers?" Marshal Bannister said tersely.

"I wanted to surprise her with a Christmas tree."

The man's mouth tightened, but Reid thought he was fighting a smile. "Was anyone at her apartment when you arrived?"

"No," Reid answered. "At least I didn't find anyone there. But the stove was hot as if someone had just used it, and there was a bubble bath waiting in the tub."

"You didn't run the bath?" Marshal Bannister asked.

Reid shot up from the table, his anger churning. "Hell, no. When I saw it, I thought maybe...never mind."

"Maybe what?"

Reid paced to the wall and turned to face the Marshal. "That maybe Lucy lied to me, that she hadn't left town. That she was seeing someone else." If the man was seeing Lucy would he fess up now?

Marshal Bannister made a low sound in his throat, then glanced at his phone. A knock sounded at the door, then another officer stepped inside, leaned over and whispered something in the man's ear. Bannister cursed, then stood.

"Excuse me, I need to make a phone call."

"Wait just a damn minute," Reid said. "What the hell is going on? The cops accused me of stalking Lucy. Why would they think I was a stalker?"

Bannister tugged at his tie, indecision on his face.

"I have a right to know," Reid said. "Did something happen to Lucy?"

"I hope not," Bannister said. "But you are free to go, Mr. Summers."

Perspiration beaded on Reid's neck. "What does that mean? You *hope* nothing happened to her?"

"Just go home," Bannister said. "And let the police take care of the situation."

"Take care of what situation?"

But Bannister didn't answer. He was already punching a number on his phone as he left the room. The guard gestured for him to follow him, then escorted Reid through security. His handcuffs were removed, and a heavyset woman in a uniform handed him his personal items.

He grabbed his phone and keys, then hurried outside.

Dammit, he didn't have a way home. He'd have to call Lance.

No, he didn't want Lance to know what had happened.

He dialed Lucy's number and prayed she'd answer and tell him that this whole mess was a big misunderstanding. But the phone rang and rang, then a recording clicked on saying her message box was full.

So she hadn't been picking up her messages?

That was odd. Lucy's car didn't crank unless she was on her cell phone.

Worry knotted his insides as he hunted for a taxi. If the police thought he was stalking Lucy, did that mean she actually had a stalker?

If she did, why hadn't she told him?

*E*ARLY MORNING SUNLIGHT GLINTED off the water, signaling another beautiful day in Delray as Lucy stepped onto her patio. She waved to the Silver Sneakers as they headed down to the beach wearing their reindeer antlers. She could hear the jingle bells on their shoes and their chatter all the way down to the jetty.

Still, Lucy felt glum. Two days until Christmas and no word from Marshal Bannister.

Her phone beeped that she had a text, and she read the message from her sister.

> Call me asap. Newspaper story this morning said police arrested a man named Emmet Roach for stalking you. What's going on? Where are you?!

Lucy jumped up and squealed. The sound must have carried in the breeze because the Silver Sneakers turned and looked at her. She waved that she was fine, then covered her mouth to stifle another cheer.

But her relief was short-lived.

If the police had Emmet, why hadn't Wallace Bannister informed her?

Don't look a gift horse in the mouth, Lucy told herself. This means you can go home!

Wallace was probably dealing with the paperwork, making sure Emmet didn't get out this time.

Knowing her sister was worried, she punched Sophie's number. Her sister answered on the first ring, her voice strained.

"Where have you been?" Sophie asked. "I've been frantic, and Reid has called a hundred times."

"Slow down, sis, everything's okay now."

"What do you mean, it's okay *now*? I thought you flew to L.A. for an audition."

"That was my cover story," Lucy said, hating that she'd been forced to lie. "I had to leave town."

"So the story about the stalker is true?"

Lucy noticed a man on the beach and squinted to make out his face, then realized she could stop searching for Emmet everywhere she turned. "Yes, I'm afraid so. But he's back in jail, so it's over."

"You mean you had a stalker and didn't tell me?"

"It happened two years ago while I was in Vegas," Lucy said. "The police finally arrested him, and I thought it was all behind me. Then a few days ago he was on a prison bus and broke out."

Lucy waved to Mae as she settled on her balcony next door with the morning obits.

"The Marshal handling my case thought it was a good idea if I left town until he was apprehended."

A long heartbeat passed. "You haven't told Reid any of this?"

"No," Lucy said. "I wanted to protect you and him in case Emmet tried to use you to get to me."

"Lucy, is this guy dangerous?" Sophie asked.

Lucy debated. "I don't know. He used to leave me gifts, forced me to go with him once. He's crazy, Sophie. He thinks he's in love with me." She hesitated. "And I don't know what prison did to him."

Another awkward moment. "Well, now he's been found, you can come home."

Lucy wanted to go back, but the Silver Sneakers waved that they'd found sand dollars to make more ornaments, and she remembered how excited they were about the Christmas talent show and knew she couldn't leave until the show was over.

"I can't, Sophie."

"Why not? Is it about Reid? Are you trying to break up with him?"

Dear God, was that what Reid thought? "No. I love Reid, but that Marshal I mentioned got me a job at this sixties-and-up community named Sunset Vista in Delray Beach and we're planning a talent show on Christmas Eve. The residents are so excited I can't just run out on them."

Sophie muttered something Lucy couldn't understand.

"I'm sorry, Sophie, don't be mad."

"I'm not mad," Sophie said. "I'm...proud of you, Lucy."

Lucy's pulse fluttered. "I have an idea. Why don't you come here for the show. We can still spend Christmas together."

"What about Reid and Lance and Maddie and Chase? And Deseree?"

Lucy twisted her hair into a ponytail. "You're right. It's not fair to ask them to leave their plans. I'll stay for the show then drive home Christmas day."

"That sounds good. And listen, Lucy," Sophie said. "If you really care about Reid, call him and explain."

Lucy hated confrontation. "I'll just surprise him when I come home."

Her phone buzzed, and she saw Bannister's number. "Hey, this is that Marshal calling. See you soon."

Sophie agreed, and she clicked to answer Bannister's call. "Hey, Wallace. My sister texted that she saw the story about Emmet's arrest in the paper."

"I know, and I'm sorry, Lucy," Marshal Bannister said. "But that was a mistake. Two officers that were watching your place did find a man in your house and arrested him. I don't know how the papers got hold of it, but they got it all wrong."

Lucy gripped her phone with sweaty fingers. "What do you mean, they got it all wrong?"

"The man they arrested claimed he was your boyfriend, but it wasn't Emmet."

"It wasn't?"

"No. Do you have a line of men chasing you, Lucy?"

If not, Emmet, then who? She sank onto the lounge chair as the truth dawned. "Oh, my God. Don't tell me you arrested Reid?"

"Yes, that was his name," Bannister said.

"Oh, no," Lucy whispered. "Where is he now?"

"I questioned him, then released him."

"Did you explain about Emmet?"

"No," Bannister said. "I figured if you'd wanted him to know you would have told him."

Dear Lord. She *should* have told him.

"Where is he now?"

"I have no idea," Bannister said. "But the problem is that Emmet is still out there."

Nausea climbed Lucy's throat as she hung up. No telling what Reid was thinking…

And that man on the beach…he could have been Emmet.

Panicked, she texted Sophie back and told her that Emmet was still on the loose, and that she wouldn't be coming home until he was.

They would have to celebrate Christmas without her.

Now, what to do about Reid? Maybe it was best to leave him in the dark until Emmet was caught.

Then she'd explain everything. She just hoped he would forgive her when she did. After all, she was trying to protect him.

That was what a girl did when she loved a man, wasn't it?

*E*MMET'S CHEST BUBBLED WITH excitement as he studied the Sunset Vista. He was going to rescue Lucy from this place.

Why, the people were almost antiques.

The plastic Santa waved to him from the lawn, giving him an idea. Maybe he and Lucy would have a Christmas wedding. Then they would honeymoon together and make a Christmas baby...

He'd heard the women on the beach discussing their upcoming Christmas Eve talent show. They were all dressing in festive attire. The show was open to the public.

It was the perfect opportunity for him to sneak inside. Now, he just needed to find something Christmasy to wear. A disguise of some sort so he could get close to Lucy.

He clapped his hands in glee and began to hum *Grandma Got Run Over By a Reindeer* as he headed into town to find a costume.

Chapter Six

REID HAD JUST STEPPED from the shower when his cell phone buzzed. He snatched it up, hoping it was Lucy, but Sophie's name flashed on the caller ID screen.

"Reid," Sophie said in a strained voice. "We need to talk."

Reid's stomach plummeted. "What's wrong?"

"Did you see the newspaper this morning?"

"No," Reid said. "I just got out of jail."

"Jail?"

"Yes," Reid said. "I went to Lucy's to surprise her with a Christmas tree — "

Okay, he was officially a bona fide sap. "— but the police busted in and arrested me."

"Oh, dear lord," Sophie whispered.

"They accused me of stalking her," Reid grumbled.

"Oh, dear lord," Sophie said.

Reid tossed his towel aside. "Stop saying that and tell me what's going on."

"First of all, I just talked to Lucy and she's okay," Sophie said.

A mixture of emotions pummeled Reid. He wanted her to be okay.

But that meant she was ignoring his calls.

"She didn't go to L.A. and there was no audition," Sophie said.

"You told me that already," Reid said tightly. "So I was right. She left me and was too chicken to tell me."

"That's not it," Sophie said, sounding annoyed.

"Then why hasn't she called me?"

"She's trying to protect you."

"Protect me?" Reid asked. "From what? I know about her dancing. What other secrets does she have?"

"Well," Sophie hedged.

Reid cursed. "Spit it out, Sophie."

"She does have a stalker," Sophie said. "That's why the police were watching her place and arrested you."

Sophie's words boomeranged in Reid's ears. Suddenly the cop's accusations, the underwear across the bed...they'd called him a pervert – it all made sense. "Who's stalking Lucy?" he asked, barely able to control the rage bubbling inside him.

"His name is Emmet Roach," Sophie explained. "He's been in prison but apparently he escaped."

"And the police think he's coming after Lucy?" Reid said, his heart hammering.

"Yes."

"Where is she, Sophie?"

"She doesn't want me to tell you," Sophie said. "She said she'll come home after he's apprehended."

Hurt mingled with worry. If she'd told him, he could have protected her. Dammit. That was the way it was supposed to work.

"I'm going after her," Reid said. "She shouldn't be alone if some psycho is after her."

"Reid –"

"Either tell me where she is or I'll find out myself."

"Reid –"

"For God's sake, tell me, Sophie. I'm not going to let Lucy go through this alone."

Tension stretched between them, then Sophie finally replied. "You're right. We should all be together on Christmas."

"Sophie –"

"Let me call Lance and my mother. If Lucy can't be here, we'll go to her tomorrow."

"All right. I'll call Maddie and Chase," Reid said. "We'll take Christmas to Lucy."

But when he hung up, his imagination went crazy with awful things that this freak might do to Lucy if he found her.

Reid didn't know if he could wait one more day to see her.

Then again, he needed the time. He still didn't have Lucy's Christmas present...

Christmas Eve

ALL AFTERNOON AND INTO the evening, Lucy felt jittery. Every time the door opened to the common room, she jumped like a reindeer caught in headlights.

Now night had set in, Christmas Eve was upon them, and the excitement over the Secret Santa gifts and the program was mounting.

Red and green streamers draped the walls, the Christmas lights glittered, and everyone had contributed party foods, decorative cupcakes and Christmas punch for the celebration after the show.

One Secret Santa gift remained on the table. Her name was on the card.

She glanced around the room where three residents were finishing decorating the stage, then through the picture glass window at the pool area, but didn't see anything suspicious.

No sign of Emmet.

But when she opened the bag, she discovered a pair of sexy red stilettos.

Fear jackknifed through her. No one here knew about her obsession with shoes.

But Emmet did. In fact, he liked trying on her shoes and underwear.

She punched Wallace Bannister's number, but his machine rolled to voice mail. "Wallace, it's me, Lucy. I'm afraid Emmet's found me. Please call me back."

She tucked the phone in her pocket, then smiled as Mae tottered toward her carrying a blueberry cobbler. "Taylor, guess what! I've got a date tonight with Harry, the man I met in the obits! He must have liked my pie after all."

Lucy laughed although guilt weighed on her for lying to these sweet people.

Moon strolled in dressed as Santa Claus. Billy and Nelda wore matching jingle bell shirts while DeEtte's shirt glittered with blinking lights. The others filed in, all dressed in festive attire, the mood jovial as they gathered for the show.

For a brief moment, she wondered what her sister was doing tonight, if she and Lance, and Reid, and Maddie and Chase were all together, sipping drinks over dinner and making toasts to the holiday.

Tears threatened, but she blinked them back. She missed her family, but she loved the people here. And she would be home soon.

Would Reid be waiting?

Christmas music piped up, and she studied the guests as they entered, one eye open for Emmet.

Sue directed everyone to take their seats, and introduced the first act.

Four Silver Sneakers, DeEtte, Ellen, Sue, and Willene performed a tap dance to Jingle Bells, the bells on their shoes ringing. Laughter and applause rang out as they finished.

Act two featured Billy and Nelda who performed their own version of Ghosts of Christmas Pasts by reenacting some of the funniest holidays they'd spent together. In the first scene, they'd spent Christmas rubbing lotion all over their six children who'd come down with chicken pox. But the first holiday was the best – they were so poor they didn't have money to buy a tree, so they chopped one down in the woods, but it was so lopsided they had to tie it to the wall with a belt to keep it upright. Then they cut Christmas cards and threaded them onto the tree for decorations.

Lucy's heart churned with emotions. She wanted the kind of love those two shared.

Next, Moon played *Here Comes Santa Claus* on his spoons while his buddy Lewis accompanied him on a set of water glasses, and Roger played the harmonica. Bradford, dressed as Santa, hung candy canes on the tree then pretended to climb up the chimney. But his big belly got stuck, and the cardboard fireplace fell apart, bringing another round of giggles.

Suddenly a commotion erupted near the back door, and Lucy went to see what it was. But when she reached the door, she noticed a woman wearing a lampshade decorated like a Christmas tree, sunglasses and a frilly bright green skirt made of netting.

The woman waved and moved toward her.

The woman had the hairiest legs she'd ever seen.

Then the truth hit her — the lampshade hat belonged to a man.

Dear God, it was Emmet!

She started to scream, but her voice died when he shoved a gun in to her side. "Hi, sweetheart, miss me?"

Lucy tensed, and saw Santa Claus climbing on stage. Maybe Santa would save her. "You won't get away with this, Emmet."

"Oh, yes, I will." He gestured toward the stage where Reba, Betty and her sisters Sheila and Shirley, and their cousins Linda, Vicky, and Janet were doing a can-can dance to *We Wish You A Merry Christmas* with Santa dancing in the middle. The crowd had joined in, everyone clapping and cheering.

"Let's go, Lucy. I've been waiting for you a long time."

"Just don't hurt any one here," Lucy whispered.

He leaned close and licked her earlobe. "Funny, Lucy, I never imagined you at a place like this."

Neither had she, but she loved the people, and she'd do anything to keep them safe..

Even if it meant going with crazy Emmet.

$\mathcal{R}$EID, LANCE AND SOPHIE, and Maddie and Chase and Deseree had slipped into the back of the room to watch the talent show, then Reid spotted Lucy with the strange looking woman in the lampshade hat.

Only it wasn't a woman. Hairy legs stretched below that green net skirt.

"That's him. He has her," he said in a low voice to Lance.

"He has a gun," Maddie screeched.

"Chase, keep Maddie out of this," Lance told Chase.

"You take care of Sophie," Reid said. "I'm going after Lucy."

"Where's Deseree?" Sophie asked.

"She's over there flirting with that man in the reindeer shirt," Chase said.

On stage, a man and several others were acting out *The Night Before Christmas* with Santa ho-ho-hoing as he handed out gifts to the few grandchildren attending the show.

Reid wove through the row of seats toward Lucy and her stalker, but Lucy saw him and gasped.

Suddenly Deseree screamed, "Lucy's in trouble, call 911!"

"Who's Lucy?" several people shouted.

The guy in the lampshade fired a shot into the air. Chaos erupted. Everyone on stage dove to the floor. Santa threw his arms over them to protect them. Women screamed and took cover under the food tables. Casseroles and punch splattered the floor.

Lucy's stalker dragged her outside by the pool. Reid pushed his way through the crowd. Lance yelled at Sophie and Maddie to stay put while he and Chase separated, running in different directions to cover the other doors.

"Stop," Reid yelled.

The lampshade jangled ornaments as the man jerked Lucy's arm.

But he saw the fight flare in Lucy's eyes. She jabbed her elbow into her stalker's side. He bellowed in pain and shock, and dropped the gun. Reid stormed him, then the two of them fought and fell into the pool.

They went under, the man's headdress floating away as Reid punched him in the face. The man fought back, but Reid was stronger and subdued him in seconds. When he dragged him to the surface, the man sputtered water.

"Let me go, I love Lucy!"

"You're going to jail," Reid shouted. "Lucy's going to marry me!"

Reid had plenty of back-up. Chase and Lance, Sophie and Maddie, Deseree, and all the residents formed a circle around the pool, shaking their fingers and fists at Lucy's stalker.

A siren wailed, tires screeched outside, then two officers raced in along with Marshall Bannister.

"He's in the pool," a white-haired man shouted.

Reid hauled Emmet to the pool steps and shoved him over the edge. When he looked up, Lucy was waiting. So was the Marshal who'd interrogated him at the police station.

"I can't believe you're here," Lucy said.

He climbed from the pool and reached for her, but she slugged him, sending him flying back into the water.

"Oh, my goodness," DeEtte tittered.

"Hon, I think we'd better have that talk about how to get a man again," Mae said.

"Maybe they do it different now," Ellen commented.

"Let me know if you two need a house," Sue shouted.

Reid flung water from him as he pulled himself out of the pool. "What the hell?"

"You could have gotten yourself killed," Lucy shouted.

But tears streamed down her face, and she was trembling.

Reid's heart melted. "I had to do something," Reid said with a smile. "I couldn't let that guy in the lampshade steal my girl."

He dragged her into his arms and closed his mouth over hers. Lucy fell into him, and kissed him back, the fear that had driven him here turning to passion.

When he finally ended the kiss, applause and cheers erupted around them.

"Well, maybe we should take man-hunting lessons from Lucy," Ellen said.

"She has a great right hook," Willene muttered.

Heat climbed Reid's cheeks when he realized that everyone was watching.

Lance was talking to the police officers on the side, obviously explaining what had happened.

Then Lucy pressed a hand to his cheek. "What was it you said about me?"

Reid narrowed his eyes. "I…hmmm…"

Lucy slapped at him. "You remember, something about me being the girl you were going to *marry*?"

"Get down on one knee," Ellen whispered.

"Tell her you love her," DeEtte yelled.

"Do you have a ring?" Nelda asked.

"Promise her forever," Willene said.

"And trips, lots of cruises," Sue added.

Reid threw his head back and laughed. "I love you, Lucy. But this is not the way I planned this."

"You planned it?" Lucy whispered.

He shrugged. "Yes. But … here goes." He dropped to one knee and took her hand in his, then removed the diamond he'd bought the day before. "Will you marry me, Lucy?"

She knelt in front of him, then looped her arms around his wet neck and nodded. "I love you, too, Reid. And yes, I'll marry you."

She kissed him so hard they fell backward into the pool. But neither of them minded.

*L*UCY LAUGHED AS SHE and Reid climbed from the pool. Someone started a chorus of *It's Beginning to Look A Lot Like Christmas*, and Sophie raced toward her and dragged her into a hug. Lance and Chase and Maddie followed, then Deseree.

"What's going on?" some of the Silver Sneakers finally asked. "We thought your name was Taylor."

Wallace motioned from the back that he had Emmet in custody. Then Lucy explained about her stalker.

"I'm sorry I put you all in danger," she said. "I didn't think Emmet would find me here."

Moon and Mae and all the people she'd come to love assured her it wasn't a problem.

"It's time to reveal your Secret Santas," Lucy said. "But first, I have to ask. Who was mine?"

Mae slipped up beside her. "We all chipped in to buy you a gift because you've done so much for us."

Tears sprang to Lucy's eyes. "I didn't do anything compared to what you've done for me. I feel like I have a new family here."

"You do, dear," Mae said.

Lucy hugged each one of them in turn, then encouraged them to reveal their Secret Santas and have refreshments, at least what they could salvage. The blueberry cobbler and punch were goners.

Lance and Sophie, Chase and Maddie and Deseree followed her and Reid back out by the pool with their drinks.

"I can't believe you all came," Lucy said.

"You should have told us the truth from the beginning," Sophie said.

"Yes," Maddie added. "We're your family, and family sticks together."

Reid threw his arm around her. "Damn right. From now on, you need anything, you come to me."

Lucy grinned, a wicked thought occurring to her. "As a matter of fact, I need to show you the Secret Santa gifts my new friends here gave me."

"Go get them," Reid said.

Lucy grabbed his hand. "No, this is something I have to show you in private."

She dragged him back to her room, removed her wet clothes, slipped into the slinky dress and stilettos the Sunset Vista residents had given her.

Only she didn't have them on for long.

Reid stripped them and made love to her just as midnight rang in signaling Christmas. Lucy curled into his arms and smiled as the red and green lights twinkled on the boats sailing across the waterway.

Tomorrow…well today, she would spend Christmas with all her family and the people she loved.

But most importantly – she would spend it with the man she was going to marry.

Other Books by Rita Herron

Love Me, Lucy is the sequel to *Sleepless in Savannah*.
If you liked *Love Me, Lucy*, then please write a review on Amazon! You can also contact Rita at www.ritaherron.com and follow her on Facebook and Twitter @ritaherron!
You also might like Rita's other sexy romantic comedies:

The Bachelor Pact

A woman places an ad to find a date, but the man who answers is an undercover cop who thinks she's a thief!

Marry Me, Maddie

A woman gives her boyfriend an ultimatum on a talk show — Marry Me or Move on! Then her brothers' best friend steps in and the battle for her hand begins!

Under the Cover

A famous marriage counselor hires a man to play her husband when her real one leaves her for a man!

Husband Hunting 101

A woman takes a class to find a husband!

Here Comes the Bride

A twin switch, a fake fiancé — a real wedding?

Single and Searching

A woman places an ad to find a date, but the man who answers is an undercover cop who thinks she's a thief!

There Goes the Groom

A jilted bride is arrested at her wedding when her fiancé dumps her and goes on the lamb!

About Rita

Multi-published, award-winning author Rita Herron fell in love with books at the ripe age of eight when she read her first Trixie Belden mystery. She has sold over sixty novels, worked for several major publishers, and loves writing romantic comedies as well as spinning dark romantic suspense tales filled with murder and mayhem.

For more on Rita and her titles, visit her at www.ritaherron.com. You can also follow her on Facebook and Twitter @ritaherron.